Jim Henson's™ DOOZERS™
Have Green Thumbs

adapted by Cordelia Evans
based on the screenplay written by Kati Rocky

Ready-to-Read

Simon Spotlight
New York   London   Toronto   Sydney   New Delhi

SIMON SPOTLIGHT
An imprint of Simon & Schuster Children's Publishing Division
1230 Avenue of the Americas, New York, New York 10020
This Simon Spotlight edition December 2015
For information about special discounts for bulk purchases, please contact
Simon & Schuster Special Sales at 1-866-506-1949 or business@simonandschuster.com.
Manufactured in the United States of America 1115 LAK
10 9 8 7 6 5 4 3 2 1
ISBN 978-1-4814-3221-4 (hc)
ISBN 978-1-4814-3220-7 (pbk)
ISBN 978-1-4814-3222-1 (eBook)

Spike and Daisy Wheel

are eating breakfast

when they hear

the Pod Squad signal!

"Time for action!"

says Flex.

"I am at the farm with

a pickle of a problem."

"We are on our way!"

says Spike.

"What is it, Flex?"

asks Molly Bolt when

the Pod Squad arrives.

"There are too many radishes on the farm," Flex explains. "There is no room for these baby radishes!"

"We use radishes in lots of ways," says Molly Bolt. "But these baby radishes still need to grow."

"We need to find them

a new home," Spike says.

Spike has an idea!

He thinks they can plant the radishes at the Doozer Depot!

"Look how much room there is," Spike says.

"It is big enough,"
says Flex, "but the soil
is too dry."

Now Molly Bolt has an idea.
They can plant the radishes
beneath her tree house!

"The space is big enough,
and the soil is moist,"
says Flex, "but it is in
the shade."

"What is wrong with

the shade?"

Molly Bolt asks.

"Plants need more than

space and soil to grow,"

Flex explains.

"They also need sunlight."

"So we need to find

a big space with

moist soil and sunlight,"

Molly Bolt says.

They decide to go ask

Professor Gimbal for help.

They find him building

a tower out of blocks.

"Can we play?" Spike asks.

"I am not just stacking blocks," says the professor. "I am designing a house that goes up, not out."

"Why?" Molly Bolt asks.

"Many Doozers could live in a tower, and it would not take up much space on the ground," Professor Gimbal explains.

"Hold your hard hats!"

cries Flex.

"We could make our radish garden go up, not out, just like your tower!"

"They would have space and sun," says Molly Bolt. "But I thought radishes need soil to grow?"

"Actually, they do not
need soil if they have
food and water,"
says Professor Gimbal.
"They usually get it from soil!"

The Pod Squad

starts to build

a garden without soil.

Then they place

the radishes in water

that has plant food in it.

The next day they

check on the radishes.

"They are growing!"

exclaims Daisy Wheel.

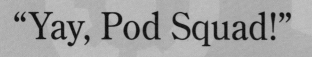

"We did it!" they cheer.

"Yay, Pod Squad!"